Growing God's Kids

BEING NICE TO OTHERS

A Book about Rudeness

CAROLYN LARSEN
ILLUSTRATED BY TIM O'CONNOR

BakerBooks
a division of Baker Publishing Group
Grand Rapids, Michigan

Published by Baker Books
a division of Baker Publishing Group
P.O. Box 6287, Grand Rapids, MI 49516-6287
www.bakerbooks.com

Printed in the United States of America

Library of Congress Cataloging-in-Publication Data
Names: Larsen, Carolyn, 1950– author.
Title: Being nice to others : a book about rudeness / Carolyn
    Larsen ; illustrated by Tim O'Connor.
Description: Grand Rapids : Baker Books, 2016. | Series:
    Growing God's kids
Identifiers: LCCN 2016011309 | ISBN 9780801009570 (pbk.)
Subjects: LCSH: Etiquette for children and teenagers—Juvenile
    literature. | Christian children—Conduct of life—Juvenile
    literature. | Courtesy—Juvenile literature.
Classification: LCC BJ1857.C5 L34 2016 | DDC 241/.671—
    dc23
LC record available at https://lccn.loc.gov/2016011309

17 18 19 20 21 22   7 6 5 4 3 2

Love is not rude, is not selfish,
and does not become angry
easily. Love does not remember
wrongs done against it.

1 CORINTHIANS 13:5

See that boy? That's Max. Most of the time he's a nice boy, but sometimes he says unkind things to people. That is called being rude. It's not cool to be rude.

My name is Leonard, and I'm Max's favorite toy.

"It's story time. Come sit down, Max," says Mrs. Roberts, the teacher.

But Max is playing with blocks and doesn't want to stop. "No!" he shouts. "I don't like story time. I don't feel like sitting down."

Mrs. Roberts is not happy. She talks to Max's mom after school.

On the way home, Mom asks Max why he was rude to his teacher.

"I was angry because I wanted to keep playing blocks," Max says.

Mom tells him, "Even when you don't want to do something, it is not OK to be rude. You need to tell Mrs. Roberts you're sorry."

The next day Max brings flowers to his teacher.

"I'm sorry I was rude to you, Mrs. Roberts. My dad and mom reminded me that I need to do what you say and not talk back," he tells her.

Love is not rude.
1 Corinthians 13:5

11

Max has been playing with his cars for hours. He has cars of many different colors and likes to line them up on the floor. He plays and plays until he starts to get tired.

When Mom says it is bedtime, Max shouts, "No! You are being mean. I won't go to bed."

"You were being rude to me," says Mom as she sits on Max's bed. "I know you're tired, but you said unkind things that hurt my feelings."

"Being tired is not an excuse for being rude," Mom says.

Max hugs his mom and tells her he's sorry.

"You're forgiven, Max. And I want you to remember what God says: We should show love to others and not be rude."

Love is not rude.
1 Corinthians 13:5

May I play with your robot, please? I've never played with one," Max's friend Hannah asks one day at a playdate.

"No. It's mine. You'll just break it. I won't let you play with it!" Max says.

Max shouts more mean things at Hannah while he runs away with the robot.

Mom comes in when she hears the shouting.

She says, "Max, your selfishness is causing you to be rude to Hannah. You need to apologize."

Mom asks Max, "How would you feel if Hannah was rude to you?"

Max must be kind if he wants to be a good friend. He tells Hannah he's sorry and lets her play with the robot.

Love is not rude.
1 Corinthians 13:5

Max likes to play with his friends. They have fun playing at the park while their moms are sitting at a picnic table nearby.

But one boy gets impatient when Max is too slow going down the slide. He shouts at Max and is rude to him.

Max gets angry when the boy says mean things. He shouts right back at the boy and calls him names. Pretty soon both boys are yelling. The other kids are afraid the boys might hit each other.

Mom hears the commotion and comes to the playground. "Let's go home, Max," she says.

Later at home, Mom and Dad tell Max that he should not be rude just because someone is rude to him. They give him suggestions on what he could do instead:

- He could walk away from a rude person.
- He could ask the rude boy to stop saying unkind things.
- He could answer back with kindness.
- He could ask an adult for help.

Love is not rude.
1 Corinthians 13:5

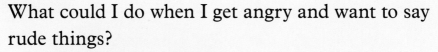

What could I do when I get angry and want to say rude things?

1. I should just walk away and calm down.
2. Remember that sometimes I must do things I don't want to do.
3. Remember that I must treat people with respect.

How can I keep from being rude when I'm tired?

1. Take a rest.
2. Ask God to help me be kind.
3. Count to ten before I speak.

How can I keep from being rude when I don't want to share my things?

1. Think about how I want to be treated.
2. Remember that saying rude things just makes my selfish behavior worse.
3. Remember that unkind words will hurt.

What can I do when someone is rude to me?
1. Remember that I do not have to answer back with rude words.
2. Remember that the other person may be tired.
3. Remember that it's more important to show love to others than to keep a fight going.

Remember

God says that the second most important commandment—after loving him—is to love others. (See Matthew 22:37–39.)

God says we show love to others by speaking kind words to them. (See Ephesians 4:29.)

God says to be careful of your words when you are angry. (See 2 Timothy 2:23–24.)

God says the best way to respond to rudeness is with kindness and patience. (See 1 Peter 3:9.)

It's never OK to be rude. Rudeness says, "I don't care about your feelings." That doesn't fit with God's command to love others and be kind to them.

Love is not rude.
1 Corinthians 13:5